Robert Louis Stevenson
was born in Edinburgh in 1850.
Though he was poor in health all his life,
he yearned for adventure and, after leaving
university, he travelled all over the world.
After living in England, Switzerland,
France, America, Tahiti and Australia,
he and his family settled in Samoa,
where Stevenson died at the age of 44.

Jonathan Mercer's woodcuts have been made
specially for Ladybird Classics. They are individually
hand-crafted from box-wood.

A catalogue record for this book is available from the British Library

Published by Ladybird Books Ltd
80 Strand London WC2R 0RL
A Penguin Company

2 4 6 8 10 9 7 5 3 1

© LADYBIRD BOOKS LTD MCMXCIV. This edition MMVIII

LADYBIRD and the device of a Ladybird are trademarks of Ladybird Books Ltd

ISBN: 978-1-84646-943-5

Printed in China

Ladybird *classics*

TREASURE ISLAND

by Robert Louis Stevenson

Retold by Joyce Faraday
Illustrated by David Frankland
Cover illustrated by Fausto Bianchi
Woodcuts by Jonathan Mercer

His name was Billy Bones

THE SEA-CHEST

I remember, as if it were yesterday, the old seaman who came to live at our inn. He was tall and strong, and a black pigtail hung down to his shoulder. His hands were rough, and he had a white scar across one cheek. His name was Billy Bones, and when he was drunk, as he often was, we were all afraid of him. He never talked to any of the sailors who called at the inn, and he paid me fourpence a month to warn him if I should ever see a sailor with one leg.

My father was ill at the time, and I was left to look after Billy Bones. He drank so much that Dr Livesey warned him that rum would kill him. But he didn't care to change his ways, and when he lay weak and helpless in his bed, he told me

5

dreadful stories of walking the plank, storms at sea and the wicked deeds of men.

He had been the mate on board the pirate ship of Captain Flint. When the captain was dying, he gave Billy Bones a map that showed where his treasure was buried. Since that day, the rest of Flint's old crew had been trying to get hold of the map. It was hidden in Billy Bones' sea-chest.

One frosty afternoon an old blind seaman, Blind Pew, called at the inn and asked to be taken to Billy Bones. He gripped Billy's hand as he left, and something passed from his hand to Billy's. Fear filled Billy's eyes when he saw what it was.

'The black spot!' he cried. 'Jim Hawkins, listen to me. This black spot means that my old shipmates are coming to get me. They're after my map, Jim! They'll kill me!' He sprang up as he spoke, and the strain and shock must have been too much. He fell dead at my feet.

Billy Bones died without paying his bills. My mother and I took some money from his sea-chest, to pay what he owed. There was also a bundle of papers, which I took for safekeeping.

That very night a gang of ruffians broke into our inn. My mother and I hid outside and watched as they searched Billy Bones' sea-chest. They took the money that remained there, but they seemed to be looking for something else. Unable to find what they wanted, they shouted and raged. I realised that they were after the bundle of papers in my pocket.

I went to Dr Livesey and his friend Squire Trelawney and told them the whole story. When we opened the bundle we found Captain Flint's treasure map. The Squire was very excited.

'Flint was the most bloodthirsty pirate that ever sailed,' he cried. 'I'll fit out a ship in Bristol! Livesey, you'll be ship's doctor. I'll take you too, Jim Hawkins – you'll be cabin boy. We'll have the best ship and the choicest crew in England. And we'll have that treasure!'

So it was that Squire Trelawney bought the *Hispaniola* and prepared her for the voyage. He needed a good crew, and took on a sailor named Long John Silver as ship's cook. His left leg was cut off close by the hip, and under his left arm he carried a crutch. He was very tall and strong.

This man was very helpful to the Squire and helped him to assemble a tough, hard-working crew. In a few weeks the *Hispaniola* was ready to sail.

He... took on a sailor named Long John Silver

THE VOYAGE

We set sail under our captain, Captain Smollett. The coxswain, Israel Hands, was an able man, and Long John Silver was a fine cook. He carried his crutch on a cord round his neck so that both his hands were free. He propped himself against the side and got on with his cooking like someone safe ashore.

We all worked well and willingly, and I often heard the crew singing as they toiled. The song was one I'd heard from old Billy Bones:

'Fifteen men on the Dead Man's Chest –
Yo-ho-ho and a bottle of rum!'

I passed many spare moments in Silver's shining galley. His parrot, Captain Flint, named after the famous pirate, swung in its cage and screeched, 'Pieces of eight! Pieces of eight! Pieces of eight!' all day long.

Silver was interesting company, full of gripping yarns of his other voyages and adventures. He was well liked by all, and the men looked up to him as a leader.

We kept a barrel of apples on deck, for the men to help themselves. One evening I went to the barrel and, finding it nearly empty, climbed inside to get an apple from the bottom. There I sat, quietly rocked by the sea.

Someone sat down on the deck, leaned against the barrel and started to speak. The words I overheard made my blood run cold. Israel Hands and Silver were planning to take over the ship once we had found the treasure. They would kill the captain and any of us who would not fall in with them! I could not believe my ears.

Suddenly there was a shout of 'Land-ho!' The men all ran to catch the first sight of land. I took the chance to jump out of the barrel and run to the safety of my friends.

Captain Smollett was telling the crew about the island. Long John Silver said that he'd been there before when his ship had put in for water. I looked at his smiling face and shuddered. I was now certain that Silver was more than a cheerful ship's cook. He was also a bloodthirsty pirate!

As soon as I could slip away I told the captain and my friends, the Squire and the doctor, what I had heard. They decided we were safe until the treasure was found. There were nineteen pirates, but only seven of us. When we were ready we would surprise them, and hope to win by catching them unprepared.

We now lay off Treasure Island. It looked a gloomy, forbidding place. The lower parts were wooded, with rocky peaks jutting above the trees. Even in the sunshine, with birds soaring above, I hated the thought of it.

It looked a gloomy, forbidding place

We were anchored in an inlet where trees came down to the water. The air was hot and still, and the men were restless and grumbling. Captain Smollett gave leave for the men to go ashore, which raised their spirits. I believe the silly fellows thought they would break their shins on treasure as soon as they landed.

Long John Silver was in charge of the two boats taking thirteen men ashore. I knew I should not be needed on board and decided to go ashore too.

MY SHORE ADVENTURE
BEGINS

I ran up the beach into the woods, glad to be free and alone. I sat quietly hidden in the bushes. Hearing voices, I moved nearer to catch the words. I could see and hear Silver bullying a sailor to join the pirates. The sailor angrily refused. Silver's answer was to plunge his dagger into the man and leave him lying dead in the forest.

I felt faint, and the whole world swam from me in a whirling mist. When I pulled myself together Silver was wiping his knife on a tuft of grass. I feared for my life if I should be found, so I ran and ran, not caring where.

I stopped at the foot of a stony hill. My eye

was caught by a movement on the hillside. I could not tell if it was a man or an animal. Here was a new danger I felt I could not face, and I began to run towards the shore.

But the creature was fast and, darting from tree to tree, he came closer. I could see now that it was a man, but so wild and strange that I was afraid. As he neared me he threw himself down and held up his hands, as if begging for mercy.

My courage returned, and I spoke to him. 'Who are you?' I asked.

'I'm poor Ben Gunn, I am,' he answered. 'It's three years since I spoke to anyone.' I had never seen such a ragged creature. He was dressed in a patchwork of tattered cloth, and his blue eyes looked startling in a face burnt black by the sun.

Babbling in a high, squeaky voice, he told me he was rich. Sometimes he spoke sense, and sometimes his words had no meaning. I felt he might be crazy after being alone for so long.

'I'm poor Ben Gunn, I am'

He said that he'd been on Captain Flint's pirate ship, and that three years before he had come back with some seamen to look for Flint's treasure. When they could not find it, the sailors went off, leaving him alone on the island. When he'd seen our ship, he'd thought that Flint had returned.

I told him that Flint was dead, but some of Flint's old shipmates were among our crew. When I spoke of Silver, his face filled with terror. I told him we should have to fight the pirates, and he promised to help us if we would take him back home with us.

Our talk was interrupted by gunfire, and we ran towards the sound. Among the trees we came upon a high wooden fence that ran round a cleared space in the forest. I saw the Union Jack flying from a log house in the clearing.

I knew that my friends must have left the ship and were defending themselves in the log house.

The battle with the pirates had begun! The *Hispaniola* lay in the inlet with the Jolly Roger at her mast. On the beach a group of drunken sailors lolled on the sand.

I parted from Ben Gunn and climbed the stockade to join my friends in the log house. They were delighted to see me, for they had feared for my safety.

Dr Livesey told me what had happened after I left the ship. The captain had decided that the time had come to fight it out with the pirates. From Flint's treasure chart he knew about the log house. Dr Livesey and one of our men had rowed ashore to find it. There was a freshwater spring by the house, and the high fence made it a good place to defend. They had then returned to the *Hispaniola* to collect the rest of the faithful crew. They had loaded a small boat with food and ammunition and made a dash for the shore.

There was a small group of pirates still on

board the ship. When they saw what was happening, they had opened fire on the little boat, and it had sunk in shallow water. The Squire's party had waded ashore, but lost half the stores and gunpowder.

The doctor was sure the pirates would soon give up the fight. He said they would get ill from too much rum, and with disease from their swampy campsite.

I told my friends what had happened to me, and of my meeting with Ben Gunn. Dr Livesey wanted to know all about him, for we clearly needed help. The leaders of our party were at their wits' end. We had little food, and the pirates could soon starve us out. I was worn out at the end of a hard day, and soon fell asleep.

I told my friends what had happened

THE ATTACK

In the morning I awoke to the sound of bustling and voices. Long John Silver himself was approaching the stockade, carrying a white flag. Captain Smollett, suspecting a trick, ordered us to be ready to fire.

Silver said he had come to make terms to end the fighting, and he was allowed to come inside the stockade. In the log house, he told the captain that the pirates intended to get the treasure. In exchange for the treasure map, he offered to take us to a safe place off the island.

Captain Smollett was not a man to make terms with pirates. Angrily, he told Silver that he and the pirates were done for. Without the map, they had no hope of finding the treasure. And with or without the treasure, not one of them could plot a course to sail the ship home. He ordered Silver to leave. Fury blazed in Silver's eyes, and with curses and threats, he disappeared into the wood.

We now prepared for the coming attack, and sat and waited in the baking heat. All at once musket shots hit the log house, and pirates leapt from the woods and climbed the stockade. Shouts and groans, shots and flashes filled the air.

I grabbed a cutlass and dashed outside to join the fight. In moments we had fought the pirates back. Those who were not killed or injured scurried to the woods for shelter.

We ran back to the log house to take stock. Two of our men had been lost, and the captain was badly injured. We were certain there would be a second attack, so we waited and watched. But all remained quiet.

In the lull, I saw Dr Livesey quietly leave the stockade. I guessed he was going to Ben Gunn.

Still no attack came, and I grew weary of waiting. The heat, the blood and the dust made me restless, and I longed to get away to a cool, fresh place. I knew the captain would never let me go, so when no one was looking I put two pistols in my pocket and slipped out.

I ran to the shore and felt the cool wind and watched the surf tumbling and tossing its foam along the beach. Climbing a hill, I could look down on the calm inlet where the *Hispaniola* lay on an unusually flat sea. In a little boat beside her, I could make out Long John Silver, talking and laughing with two men on the ship. No words reached me, but the screeching of Silver's parrot was carried on the wind.

About sundown, Silver shoved off for shore and the two men left on board went below deck. I was sure that if the pirates could not find the treasure they would sail away without us. A plan began to grow in my mind.

I could look down on the calm inlet

Ben Gunn had told me that he had made a boat and hidden it near the shore. If I could get to the *Hispaniola,* I could cut her anchor ropes. She would drift away to another part of the shore, and the pirates would be unable to escape from the island.

I searched in the bushes and, to my joy, found the hidden boat. It was made of goatskin, stretched over a wooden frame, but it was so flimsy I wondered if it were strong enough to hold me.

With darkness, fog crept into the inlet. It was a perfect night for my plan. I pushed away from the shore and drifted silently towards the *Hispaniola.*

MY SEA ADVENTURE
BEGINS

As I came alongside the ship I could hear
loud, drunken voices. Israel Hands was shouting
at another man. They were not only the worse
for rum, it was plain that they were also angry.
On the shore I could see the glow of the fire in
the pirates' camp. Someone there was singing the
song I'd heard so often before:

'Fifteen men on the Dead Man's Chest –
  Yo-ho-ho and a bottle of rum!
  Drink and the devil had done for the rest –
  Yo-ho-ho and a bottle of rum!'

Strand by strand, I cut the anchor rope, and
the ship began to swing and slide away to the
open sea. As she slid past me, I could see into

the cabin. Israel Hands and the ship's watchman were fighting. They were too busy to feel the movement of the ship. I lay flat in my little boat, praying that I should not be seen.

For hours, as the sea grew rough again, I was tossed on the waves. I must have slept, for it was broad daylight when I awoke. My boat had drifted along the coast, but I could see no landing place under the rocky cliffs. I could only let my boat drift on and hope to find a sandy shore. The hot sun and the salt from the sea spray had given me a raging thirst. I wanted to be on shore in the cool shade of the trees.

As I rounded a headland, the sight before me made me forget my cares. No more than half a mile away lay the *Hispaniola*! Her sails were set, but by the way she turned and drifted, it was clear no one was steering her. If the pirates were drunk and I could get aboard, I might be able to capture the ship!

For hours... I was tossed on the waves

I paddled fast, but with the wind filling her sails, the *Hispaniola* kept her lead. At last I had my chance. The breeze fell, and she turned in the current and stopped. I came alongside and leapt aboard. The wind took her sails, and she rushed down on a wave and sank my little boat. I had no way of escape now. I moved quietly on the deck among empty bottles. Not a soul was to be seen.

At length I saw two pirates. One was clearly dead, lying on the bloodstained deck. The other was Israel Hands, wounded and groaning and unable to stand. When he saw me he begged for brandy to ease his pain. I went below into the wrecked cabin to find some, and after a drink he seemed stronger.

I agreed to give Hands food and to patch up his wounds, if he would tell me how to steer the ship into a safe harbour. For the time being, we needed each other. But I did not trust his odd smile as he watched me.

He asked me to fetch some wine from the cabin, and when he thought I had gone below, he staggered painfully across the deck and picked up a knife he had hidden in his jacket. This was all I needed to know. Hands was now armed, and I knew he meant to kill me as soon as we brought the ship ashore.

A dagger was in his right hand

IN THE ENEMY'S CAMP

The beaching was difficult. It took all my care, for I did not want to damage the ship, and so I was too busy to keep watch on Hands all the time. Suddenly I was aware of danger. Perhaps I had heard a creak or seen a shadow moving with the tail of my eye, but sure enough, when I looked round, there was Hands, already halfway towards me. A dagger was in his right hand.

I dashed away and pulled a pistol from my pocket. Turning, I took aim and fired. There was no flash, no sound. The powder was wet with seawater.

The ship gave a sudden lurch as she hit the shore, and we were both thrown off our feet. Before Hands could stand again, I had climbed the mast. Safe for the moment, I sat in the rigging and put dry powder in my pistols. Hands was slowly coming up the mast after me, his dagger between his teeth.

'One more step, Mr Hands,' I called, 'and I'll blow your brains out!' He stopped and in a flash flung his dagger. I felt a sharp pain and found myself pinned to the mast by the shoulder. The sudden pain and shock made me fire both my pistols. With a cry, Israel Hands fell headfirst into the water.

I felt sick and faint and shut my eyes until I became calm. When I had freed myself, I found that the wound was not very deep, in spite of the blood that ran down my arm. In the cabin I found bandages to bind up my wound.

It was sunset, and I waded ashore. All I wanted was to be back with my friends. I hoped that the capture of the *Hispaniola* would be enough for them to forgive me for having left them.

The moon helped me to find my way to the stockade. I walked carefully and silently and dropped over the fence. There was no sound. The man on watch had not heard me. I crept to the log house and stepped inside.

Suddenly a shrill voice rang out in the darkness: 'Pieces of eight! Pieces of eight! Pieces of eight!' Silver's parrot!

Instead of finding my friends, I had come face to face with the pirates – and capture. By the light of a flaming torch, I saw Silver and the five men who were still alive.

There was no sign of my friends, and my first thought was that they had all been killed. But I soon learned that this was not so.

While I had been away, Dr Livesey had gone to the pirates and told them that, because the ship had gone, he and his party had given up the search for treasure. The log house and everything in it, even the treasure map, was handed over to the pirates and my friends had walked out into the woods.

This news puzzled me. I could not understand why they had given up without a fight.

Long John Silver was still the pirate leader, but he seemed less cheerful than before. It was clear that the men did not obey him willingly. If they should pick a new leader, Silver knew that they would kill him. His only hope of being saved was to be on Captain Smollett's side.

He promised to protect me from the pirates, if I would put in a good word for him with the captain. But if the pirates guessed he had changed sides, I knew they would finish us both. Our lives depended on keeping our plan secret.

The next morning Dr Livesey came to the log house to see to the sick and wounded. He was surprised to see me with the pirates, but he said nothing. He went on his rounds, giving out medicine and dressing wounds. When he had

He promised to protect me

finished, he asked to speak to me alone.

The doctor spoke harshly to me at first, telling me it was cowardly to have joined the pirates. But when I told him of all that had happened to me, his view quickly changed.

When he heard that the *Hispaniola* was safe, the doctor's eyes opened wide in amazement. I told him of Silver's danger, and he agreed to take him home with us if Silver would keep me safe. We were in a tight corner, and it looked as if there was little hope of getting out of it. At last the doctor shook my hand and said he was off to get help.

By now the pirates were growing restless to go out and find the treasure. But there was a question in Silver's mind – he wondered why the treasure map should have been given to him. He knew that somewhere there must be a trick, and he dared not let the pirates guess his thoughts.

As we sat round the fire, eating breakfast, Silver chatted away, telling the pirates how rich they would all be when they had found the treasure. He painted such a picture that I thought he believed his own words.

We set out to find Captain Flint's treasure

THE TREASURE HUNT

With picks and shovels, we set out to find Captain Flint's treasure. The men were armed to the teeth. Silver had two guns and a cutlass. As I was a prisoner, I had a rope tied round my waist. Silver held the other end. In spite of his promise to keep me safe, I did not trust him.

As we went, the men talked about the chart. On the back of it was written:

> 'Tall tree, Spy-glass Shoulder, bearing a point
>   to the N. of N.N.E.
> Skeleton Island E.S.E. and by E.
>   Ten feet.'

So we were looking for a tall tree on a hill. The men were in high spirits, and Silver and I could not keep up with them.

41

Suddenly there was a shout from one of the men in front. The others ran towards him, full of hope. But it was not treasure he had found. At the foot of the tree lay a human skeleton.

The men looked down in horror. The few rags of clothing that hung on the bones showed that the man had been a sailor. The skeleton was stretched out straight, the feet pointing one way and the arms, raised above the head, pointing in the opposite direction.

'This here's one of Flint's little jokes!' cried Silver. 'These bones point E.S.E. and by E. This is one of the men he killed, and he's laid him here to point the way!'

The men felt a chill in their hearts, for they had all lived in fear of Flint. 'But he's dead,' said one of them.

'Aye, sure enough, he's dead and gone below,' said another pirate. 'But if ever a ghost walked, it would be Flint's.'

'Aye,' said a third man. 'I tell you, I don't like to hear "Fifteen Men" sung now, for it was the only song he ever sang.'

Silver put an end to their talk and we moved on, but I noticed that now the men spoke softly and kept together. Just the thought of Flint was enough to fill them with terror.

At the top of the hill we rested. In whispers, the men still talked of Flint.

'Ah, well,' said Silver, 'you praise your stars he's dead.'

Suddenly, from the trees ahead, a thin, trembling voice struck up the well-known song:

'Fifteen men on the Dead Man's Chest –
Yo-ho-ho and a bottle of rum!'

I have never seen men so dreadfully affected as these pirates. The men were rooted to the spot. The colour drained from their faces as they stared ahead in terror. Even Silver was shaking, but he was the first to pull himself together.

'I'm here to get that treasure!' he roared.
'I was never feared of Flint in his life, and by
the Powers, I'll face him dead!'

Long John Silver gave them all fresh heart,
and they picked up their tools and set off again.

We soon saw ahead a huge tree that stood high
above the others. The thought of what lay near
that tree made the men's fears fade, and they
moved faster. Silver hobbled on his crutch.
I could tell from the evil in his eyes that, if he got
his hands on the gold, he would cut all our
throats and sail away.

The men now broke into a run, but not for
long. They had come to the edge of a pit. At the
bottom lay bits of wood and the broken handle of
a pickaxe. It was clear for all to see that the
treasure had gone!

The pirates jumped down into the hole and
began to dig with their hands. Silver knew that
they would turn on him at any moment.

The treasure had gone!

'We're in a tight spot, Jim,' he whispered.
The look of hate in his eyes had gone. With
the pirates against him, he needed me again.
Once more he had changed sides.

The pirates scrambled out of the pit and stood
facing Silver and me. The leader raised his arm
to charge, but before a blow was struck, three
musket shots rang out and two pirates fell. The
three men left ran for their lives. From out of the
wood ran the doctor and Ben Gunn, who had
saved us in the nick of time.

LAST WORDS

Silver and I were taken to Ben Gunn's cave, where the rest of our party was waiting. It was a happy moment for me to see all my friends again. And my friends were glad to move out of the log house to the safety of Gunn's cave.

We now learned the answer to the question that had puzzled Silver and me. Dr Livesey had found out that Ben Gunn, alone on the island for so long, had discovered the treasure and taken it to his cave. The map, then, was useless.

That morning, Ben Gunn had watched from the woods as the pirates set out to seek the treasure. It was *his* voice that had struck terror into their hearts with his ghostly song!

That night the captain, still weak from

his wounds, along with Squire Trelawney, Dr Livesey and the rest of us, feasted and laughed and rested. Long John Silver, smiling quietly, became the polite and willing seaman I had first known.

The next day we began to pack the treasure into sacks, in preparation for loading it aboard the *Hispaniola*. There was a great mass of gold coins, from every part of the world, and transporting it all was a difficult task. It took several days to move this great fortune. With the treasure stowed, and plenty of water, we were ready to weigh anchor and set sail for home.

Though we were not certain of their whereabouts, we knew there were three pirates still on the island. After some deliberation, we decided to leave them a good stock of food, along with some medicine, clothing and tools, so that they could last until some ship found them.

And so we set sail. I cannot express the joy

We decided to leave them food

I felt as I watched Treasure Island melt into the distance and disappear over the horizon.

We had not enough crew to sail the ship home and so we made for the nearest port in South America to find some extra men. We dropped anchor and went ashore, happy to be once again in a bright, busy place.

It was nearly dawn when the doctor, the Squire and I returned to the *Hispaniola.* Ben Gunn met us and told us that Silver had left the ship. He had taken a small amount of the treasure and gone. We were all glad to be rid of him. Our one wish now was to reach Bristol safely.

We had a good voyage home. When we arrived, we shared out the treasure and settled back into our daily lives. Ben Gunn got a thousand pounds, which he spent or lost in less than three weeks. He was given a little job in the village, and he still sings in the church choir every Sunday.

Of Long John Silver we never heard anything again, and he has gone right out of my life. But sometimes, in a bad dream, I fancy I hear his parrot, Captain Flint, still screeching, 'Pieces of eight! Pieces of eight! Pieces of eight!'